Another Helping of CHIPS

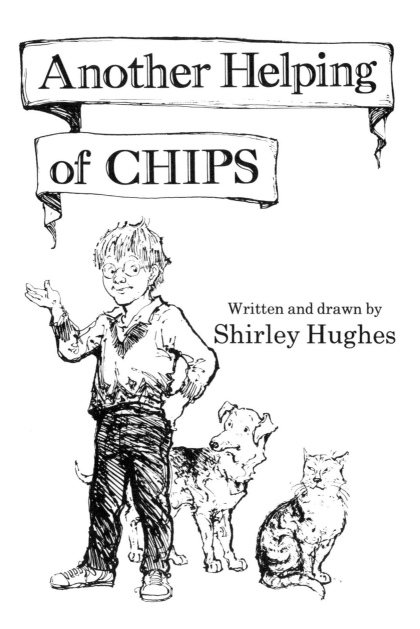

Written and drawn by
Shirley Hughes

Lothrop, Lee & Shepard Books
New York

ALSO BY SHIRLEY HUGHES
Chips and Jessie

First U.S. Edition 1987 1 2 3 4 5 6 7 8 9 10

Library of Congress Cataloging in Publication Data   Hughes, Shirley.   Another helping of chips.   Summary: Four humorous episodes in the continuing adventures of Chips and his friend Jessie, who must deal with spring cleaning, an obnoxious visiting relative, a rambunctious kitten, and the excitement of Christmas. Two episodes are presented in comic strip format and two as a combination of text and comics.   [1. Humorous stories. 2. Cartoons and comics]   I. Title.
PZ7.H87395An   1987   [E]   86-20958   ISBN 0-688-06871-5   ISBN 0-688-06872-3 (lib. bdg.)

Dear All,

These stories are all about US. Our friend, Shirley Hughes, who has done one book about us already, has written them down and drawn lots of pictures to go with them.

Of course, there are some other people in the book, too, like my little sister, Gloria, (but she can't talk properly yet, so she's not much use) and my mum and grandpa. (My dad's a cook on a big ship and has to be away a lot, so it's lucky for me that there's another man about the house.) There are people like Fred Laski, Winston, Big Joan, Little Joan and Spud Ellis, who are in our class at school. Oh, and there's Jessie's dog, Barkis, and our cat, Albert, but they've been getting a bit big-headed and cheeky lately, if you ask me.

I wanted Shirley to do a story in which Jessie and I got into a space capsule and zoomed off into the galaxies and had adventures with creatures

from other planets. But, the way it's turned out, we are stuck at home in Mallard Street, as usual, with Barkis and Albert. Still, as I said before, we *are* the most important people in the book. So get ready for some really great stories about . . .

CONTENTS

SPRING FEVER!

Perfect peace ... rudely shattered!

8

But help is on the way . . .

From now on I'm going to do just as I want!

No more proper meals. You can be as messy as you like.

I've got to go home for supper now, Chips.

Goodnight, Jessie!

Just think of it, Albert, No more awful spring-cleaning!

Chips! It's supper-time!

I'm not coming!

Come on, it's sausages and beans, your favourite.

Albert and I are staying HERE!

But it'll be dark soon!

NO!

Oh, very well, then!

Leave us alone. We're camping!

Slam!

Good. She's gone indoors!

10

Later that night:

11

Mum? Are you awake?

Come on, inside!

Is that you, Chips?

We've decided not to camp out, after all!

Albert was a bit NERVOUS of the dark.

...so I think perhaps we'll wait till the summer comes.

Good idea, Chips. I've finished the spring-cleaning, anyway.

How are you liking living in a tent, Chips?

It must be such FUN!

Well, er, now that things are back to normal at home, Albert and I have decided to POSTPONE our plans for a little while...

COUSIN WALDO'S VISIT

One day Chips's grown-up Cousin Waldo arrived on a visit. He brought a lot of luggage with him because he intended to stay for quite a long time. Chips wasn't at all pleased. He didn't like Cousin Waldo much, even though he *was* a relation. Chips didn't care for his jokes, or his loud laugh, or the way his moustache joined on to his side-whiskers, somewhere in the middle of his wide cheeks.

Although Cousin Waldo had no children of his own, he thought that he got on very well with other people's. Whenever he met Chips, he liked to pretend that the two of them were cowboys and rode the range together. Chips was too polite to tell Cousin Waldo that he wasn't interested in cowboys.

Oh, er, hello, Cousin Waldo.

Howdy, pardner! Great to see you, ol' pal!

Cousin Waldo would grab hold of Gloria and toss her into the air, then tickle her under the chin and bounce her up and down on his lap.

This made her scream with delight at first, but soon made her feel sick and rather cross, so that Mum had to hurry her off to bed.

Upsa daisy!

chooka, chooka, choo!

14

Chips had had to move out of his bedroom to make room for Cousin Waldo. This meant moving in with Gloria and having to put his light out early, instead of reading or playing with his toy space-craft. But on the first evening of Cousin Waldo's visit Chips had to spend so long fighting imaginary frontier battles, crouching behind chairs and shooting at Redskins, that he felt quite worn out and was glad to get to bed early.

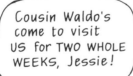

Chips grumbled a lot about Cousin Waldo to Jessie. She was very sympathetic.

By the next day Cousin Waldo had unpacked
and settled into Chips's bedroom. He also settled
comfortably on to the sofa where Chips and
Grandpa usually sat to watch television. Cousin
Waldo liked television, too, but not the same
programmes as they did. He took up a great deal of
space on the sofa, leaning forward to peer at the
set because he was short-sighted. He didn't like
wearing his glasses because he thought they spoilt
his good looks.

When at last it was time for
Chips's and Grandpa's favourite
programme, Cousin Waldo
jumped up, turned off the set
and suggested a run round the
block. Grandpa retired silently
behind his newspaper. Chips
tried to pretend that he had
some school work to get on
with, but it was no good.

We shouldn't
be sitting here,
idly watching
TV !

CLICK!

Let's have
some ACTION !

Well, er, I've
got this holiday
project to do...

16

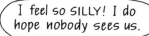

He soon found himself pounding along the pavement behind Cousin Waldo, hoping very much that they wouldn't meet Jessie or any of his other friends.

Cousin Waldo was very keen on keeping fit. He unpacked from his suitcase a brightly-coloured contraption made of wires and springs which he used in the early morning for strengthening his arms.

After this he did lots of press-ups, knee-bends, jumps and touching toes. Finally he lay on the floor and kicked his legs in the air.

The whole household was woken by the thumps and bangs.

17

Remember, only one teaspoonful of oil and **NO** sugar!

Even more than wanting to be fit, Cousin Waldo wanted to keep slim. He had a long list of things he must *never* eat in case they made him fat. He gave Mum strict instructions about meals and hovered about in the kitchen when she was cooking to check that she wasn't doing it all wrong.

Family meals had to be just as Cousin Waldo wanted them. Chips and Grandpa began to groan inwardly at the sight of raw vegetables.

Anyone'd think we were rabbits.

Oh dear, not lettuce and grated carrots AGAIN!

Delicious! And so few calories!

One evening Mum took pity on them both and cooked a huge bowl of spaghetti with fried onions and cheese and tomato sauce.

When Cousin Waldo sniffed the delicious smell of it wafting over his cucumber salad, he said that perhaps a *teeny-weeny*, little helping of spaghetti wouldn't do him any harm, just this once. And, although he held up his hands in horror at the sight of the apple-pie and ice-cream to follow, he let himself be persuaded into having quite a large portion.

mmmm!

Later that evening Chips noticed that the rest of the apple pie had mysteriously disappeared from the fridge, which was a pity, as he was hoping that Mum would let him finish it up for a treat.

Cousin Waldo often weighed himself
on the bathroom scales, but afterwards
he never seemed very cheerful.
The jumps and bangs in the early
morning increased until they
fairly shook the house.

The runs around the block became longer and
more energetic. He even tried doing disco-dancing
in the back garden wearing his red track-suit. But
a glimpse of Jessie and Fred Laski, peeping over
the hedge in fits of giggles, put him off.

As Cousin Waldo's visit dragged on, Chips began to feel desperate. He was missing all his favourite television programmes and he was sick to death of having to play Cowboys and Redskins every day after tea. The last straw came over the chocolate cake. Mum made it specially to cheer him up. It was his favourite.

All the time Mum was cooking it, Cousin Waldo hung about in the kitchen, fussing and offering disapproving advice.

But when suppertime came, after chewing thoughtfully for a while on a stick of celery, Cousin Waldo said that he might just try one little slice of cake. Then Chips had to watch grimly as half the cake disappeared into Cousin Waldo's mouth.

Chips was in a dangerous mood that evening. He raged against Cousin Waldo in the bathroom as he brushed his teeth. Luckily Albert was the only one who could hear, and he seemed sympathetic.

Chips slammed down his toothbrush, looking for some way to vent his fury. Albert wisely jumped to safety on to the side of the bath. Chips aimed a savage kick at the bathroom scales.

Hey, steady on!

Take THAT, you!

The scales spun half-way across the bathroom and hit the wall. The whole top fell off. Chips stared at the scales. The figures were on a sort of clock-face which showed you your weight.

With the top off, Chips could see right inside the scales. He took a good look. Hastily he fitted the top on again. It was a bit loose, but not enough to notice. Chips went off to bed looking thoughtful. He had an idea.

Hmm!

He's up to something, mark my words.

Very early next morning, before anyone was awake, Chips slipped into the bathroom and took the scales into his bedroom. The top came off again quite easily.

With the help of some white paint and black ink, Chips carefully changed the numbers on the higher register of the scale. He changed 65 kilos to 70, 70 to 75, and so on. It was a neat job. When he had finished and had fitted the top back on again, the changes were hardly noticeable, especially to someone who wasn't wearing their glasses.

By the time everyone woke up the scales were safely back in the bathroom. Chips was loitering about carelessly on the landing when Cousin Waldo, having finished his exercises, went into the bathroom for his morning shower. When he came out again, he was grim-faced.

Are you feeling all right, Waldo?

Gloom hung over the breakfast table. Cousin Waldo didn't crack any of his usual jokes. When Mum asked if he wasn't feeling well, he shook his head impatiently. At lunchtime he picked at a lettuce leaf, and at teatime he got quite annoyed when he was offered what was left of the chocolate cake.

Later Chips saw him examining himself sideways in the hall mirror.

Next morning Cousin Waldo came out of the bathroom with a face like a thunder cloud. Instead of coming downstairs for breakfast he went straight into his room without a word.

GLOOM

Peeping round the half-open door, Chips saw a sight which made his heart leap with joy. Cousin Waldo was packing!

Soon they were all in the hall. Cousin Waldo had his luggage ready and was waiting for a taxi to take him to the station.

No, really, I must be off. The change of diet doesn't suit me. You see, I've got this very SENSITIVE DIGESTION.

Won't you stay a little longer, Waldo?

They all went out on to the pavement to wave good-bye.

"I wonder why he left so suddenly?" said Mum, glancing thoughtfully at Chips.

"Shall I go and put my things back in my own room?" said Chips, quickly changing the subject.

That evening Chips and Grandpa settled down on the sofa to watch their favourite television programme.

"It's an odd thing," remarked Grandpa, "but today I noticed that something had happened to the bathroom scales."

Chips turned pink and tried to look innocent.

"Luckily the top was loose," Grandpa went on, "so I was able to get the figures back to normal." He filled his pipe thoughtfully. "Of course, it was very silly of whoever did it, but now they're put right, I don't suppose anyone will notice the difference."

Chips wriggled back into the sofa and said nothing. Silently they both turned their attention to the programme. The delicious smell of onions frying for supper floated in from the kitchen.

THE GHOST
IN THE
SHOPPING-BAG

Help,
it's a ghost!
I'm being
haunted!

One day Chips's mum asked him to run down to the fish-shop to get some fish for dinner.

Mrs Harris ran the fish-shop. She was a very friendly lady. She had purple hands and red arms because she slapped freezing cold bits of fish about all day on a wet marble slab.

A large mackerel lay on the slab, in a bed of parsley. It looked at Chips with round, dead, fishy eyes. Chips looked back uncertainly.

"Nice bit of mackerel, dear?" said Mrs Harris. And she whisked up the fish, chopped off its head and plonked it on to the scales before you could say "knife". Then she wrapped it up in newspaper and handed it to Chips.

Chips paid Mrs Harris and started off home, swinging his shopping-bag and trying hard not to think too much about the look in the fish's eye.

On the way home
Chips went past the
Adventure Playground.
Jessie and Fred Laski
and some other friends
were sitting up on
the high beam, dangling
their legs. When they
called out to him,
Chips couldn't resist
stopping to play, just
for a little while.

Chips carefully put down the
shopping-bag under a seat
and climbed up to join them.

30

They balanced along the beam,

and swung
on ropes,

and fooled about
on the logs.

Oh, help, I'm late!

Yeah, I'm getting hungry.

It must be nearly dinner-time.

It was when they were hanging upside-down on the bars, that Chips suddenly remembered the time.

Shouting good-bye to everyone, he picked up the shopping-bag and ran all the way home.

Mum was in rather a cross mood when he arrived. Gloria had had her dinner already. She was eating a chocolate biscuit and had got most of it on to her cheeks and into her hair. Mum had sat her on the draining-board and was trying to clean her up.

"You're so late, Chips!" said Mum. "I was wondering where you'd got to!"

Chips dumped the shopping-bag down on the kitchen table. Then a very strange thing happened. The shopping-bag started to move! First it shook a little, then it wobbled, then it moved across the table and teetered on the edge! They all stared at it, open-mouthed.

"The mackerel's come alive!" said Chips, his voice a terrified squeak. "I didn't like the way it looked at me in the shop!"

The shopping-bag leaned over sideways. It seemed to hover on the edge of the table. Then it fell to the floor with a heavy plop. A pair of shining eyes looked out from the dark inside. But they weren't fishy eyes. A pair of whiskers and a small furry face appeared.

"It's a kitten!" cried Chips.

It was a kitten all right, a real one. It was pale grey with shadowy stripes and it smelt strongly of fish. It wandered calmly out of the bag and started to pat what was left of the newspaper parcel in an interested way. It sniffed all around. Then it walked up to Chips's feet and gave a tiny mew.

"Where on earth did it come from?" said Mum, astonished. "Did you bring it home?" she asked Chips sternly.

"No, I didn't, honest." said Chips. He got down on the floor and stroked the kitten very gently under its chin. The kitten purred loudly.

"You must have put that bag down somewhere on the way home, for a kitten to have got into it," said Mum. "What's more," she grumbled, "it seems to have eaten most of the fish!" Chips had to admit that he had stopped off for a while at the Adventure Playground.

"It must be a stray," said Mum. "Perhaps some thoughtless person abandoned it at the Playground. And, of course, it was attracted into the bag by the smell of fish. Well, one thing is certain. It's not going to make itself at home here!"

I only stopped at the playground for about a MINUTE, honestly!

It's such a SWEET kitten!

Puddy tat!

We've got one cat already!

Nevertheless, the kitten played happily under the table while they had dinner (the remains of yesterday's cold meat). It invented a game with Chips's shoe laces. Afterwards, Chips secretly gave it what was left on his plate. The kitten ate greedily, pushing the food about with its little pink tongue.

It was at this moment that Albert appeared.

Here you are, kitty!

Eat it up quickly, and don't tell anybody, will you?

He came strolling in from the garden, sniffing the air. When he saw the kitten, he stopped dead and all his fur stood out. He crouched down, glaring and swishing his tail angrily.

"It's all right, Albert," said Chips reassuringly. "It's only a little kitten." And he hurriedly put down another plateful of remains.

But Albert wasn't reassured. He gulped his food, glancing round warily between bites. Then he stalked off, without a word to anybody.

> Don't be cross, Albert. You were a little kitten once, you know.

"Poor Albert, I think he's jealous," said Chips.

"That kitten's got to go," said Mum. "One cat's quite enough in this house!"

"But where's it going to go *to*?" asked Chips.

"You'll have to try and find its owner," said Mum firmly.

So the next day, when Jessie came round, they spent the morning carefully writing out notices. Jessie helped with some of the spelling.

FOUND!

at the
Beale Street
Adventure Playground
A gray ¢Kitten
Very frendly
Will the owner please ~~pleese~~
Contact:
Mr Chips Hall
49 Mallard Street

> With an 'ea' I think, Chips.

> How do you spell 'Beale', Jessie?

That afternoon they went round putting up all the notices: one by the front gate, one at the Adventure Playground and the others on some trees, fences and lamp-posts in between.

They gave the last one to Mrs Harris and asked if she would kindly put it up in her shop.

When they returned, they found the kitten quite
at home. It was in a lively mood, jumping
sideways, stiff-legged, into patches of sunlight on
the floor.

It burrowed under the edge of
the rug, then tried to run up the
back of an arm-chair.

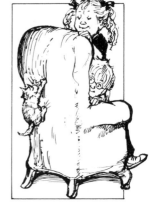

When they tied a crumpled piece of paper on to
a long string, the kitten had a great time, lying in
wait and then tossing it into the air and bicycling
on it with its back paws.

Chips, too, was enjoying himself so much that he quite forgot about Albert until long after Jessie had gone home.

After he had shut the kitten in the kitchen with a saucer of milk and a cosy bed made out of a cardboard box, Chips went upstairs. Albert was sitting hunched up in the middle of his bed.

Oh, Albert, you're not cross, are you?

tickle tickle

You ARE in a bad mood!

Chips tickled him fondly behind the ears. But Albert sniffed Chips's fingers and jumped off the bed at once.

Albert spent the evening on the front door mat, looking haughty and distant, until somebody let him out.

Nobody claimed the kitten. Chips went round every day, checking that the notices were still there, but nothing happened.

Secretly Chips was rather pleased. Having the kitten was fun and he spent a lot of time playing with it. So did Gloria. But Albert found the kitten very annoying. It ate the food on his plate and fell asleep on his special cushion.

It kept pretending that the tip of Albert's tail was a mouse and pouncing on it.

Then Albert would hiss at the kitten and box its ears, but the kitten didn't seem to care a bit.

If we can't find the kitten's owner soon, it'll just have to go to the Cats' Home.

But it might not like it there!

Mum said that the kitten had to go. Chips protested, but Mum had made up her mind. Chips went round asking all his friends if they would like to adopt a kitten. They all thought it was a great idea.

Would you like to adopt a kitten, Fred?

Sure.

A kitten? Oh, goody. I'll ask my mum.

I've always wanted a kitten!

It's a grey one...

Sweet! My favourite colour!

... and my mum says that if we can't find a place for it, it'll have to go to the Cats' Home, Jessie.

Oh, you can't do that! I'll ask at home.

It's ever so well behaved — most of the time.

Kittens are GREAT!

43

But their mums and dads thought differently.

44

"If only you could tell us where you came from," Chips said to the kitten. But the kitten seemed to have made itself quite at home where it was.

Albert stayed at home less and less. In the end he only came in for his meals.

He spent most of his time sitting on the high wall at the end of the garden. It was the only place where he could get away from the kitten.

Then one night, when Chips called him for his supper, Albert didn't come in at all.

Chips went down the garden, calling and searching. He looked in all Albert's favourite places. He even went down the street, peering over walls, behind dustbins and into other people's gardens, until it was quite dark.

Chips was very uneasy when he went to bed, and even more upset the next day when Albert didn't appear.

"It's because of the kitten!" said Chips. "Albert must have thought I didn't like him any more." And suddenly Chips felt terribly sad.

That afternoon he didn't play with the kitten at all. Instead he made another notice, a huge one. When it was finished, some of the letters were running into each other because of the tears which trickled down Chips's cheeks and on to the paper.

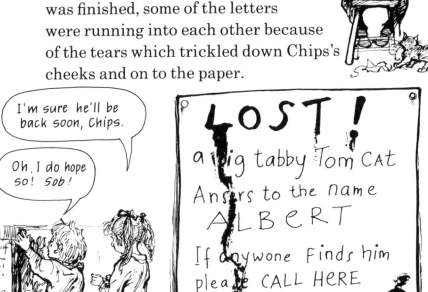

I'm sure he'll be back soon, Chips.

Oh, I do hope so! Sob!

LOST !
a big tabby Tom CAT
Ansers to the name
ALBERT
If anywone Finds him
please CALL HERE
A WONce
BIG REWARD
OFFERED!

Jessie helped him pin it up on the front gate, beside the other notice. The bit about the big reward wasn't quite true because Chips only had 32p in his money-box, but he was too desperate to care.

No news was heard of Albert. Chips couldn't sleep at night for thinking of him. Perhaps he had wandered far away and couldn't find the way back? Or had even been run over by a car? But that was too terrible to imagine.

> Perhaps something awful's happened to him.

Poor Chips became sadder and sadder. Even Mum had to admit that perhaps something had happened to Albert. In the end, there was only one thing she could think of that would cheer Chips up. She said that if by *any* chance Albert didn't come back, they could keep the kitten.

> Perhaps he won't ever come back!

> Never mind, Chips. If he doesn't turn up, I suppose we'll have to keep the kitten.

The kitten was fast asleep in the middle of a newspaper. Chips took it on his lap. It stretched out its paws and purred loudly. Chips felt a little bit comforted, but not very. The kitten was a lot of fun, but Albert was his oldest friend.

> You're very sweet, but you're not the same as Albert.

49

Here you are, Chips. You can give the kitten a treat.

Puddy tat!

The next day, after school, when Chips was mooching aimlessly about the house, Mum told him to go and buy some bits of fish for the kitten's supper.

Chips took the shopping-bag and walked slowly down to Mrs Harris's shop. Mrs Harris was just about to close. Chips's 'FOUND' notice was still pinned up by the till.

"We may be going to keep the kitten, after all," Chips told her sadly.

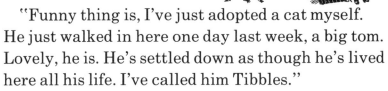

Nobody claimed him yet?

"Well, it's nice that you're going to give it a good home," said Mrs Harris.

"Funny thing is, I've just adopted a cat myself. He just walked in here one day last week, a big tom. Lovely, he is. He's settled down as though he's lived here all his life. I've called him Tibbles."

Chips's heart began to beat very fast. He asked Mrs Harris if he could please see Tibbles. So, after locking up the shop, she led the way to her flat upstairs.

Oh, Mrs Harris, please may I see him?

The flat was very warm and cosy and smelt of fish. There were a great many plants and a big velvet sofa pulled up to the fire. There, lying back like an Emperor among the cushions, was Albert.

"Oh Albert! Is it really you?" cried Chips. And he threw himself on to Mrs Harris's sofa and gave Albert a big joyful hug. Albert looked at him sideways out of one lazy eye.

We thought he'd gone for ever, Mrs Harris.

Well, imagine that!

Mrs Harris was very nice when Chips explained about Tibbles really being Albert, and said that of course they must have him back at once.

So Chips took Albert home. He had a difficult time getting him there. At first, Albert refused to get into the shopping-bag, so Chips had to carry him. He was very heavy, and kept trying to struggle out of Chips's arms.

Would you like a ride in this nice shopping-bag?

That thing? Not likely.

You HAVE put on weight!

Stop it, Albert!

In the end Chips had to wrap him up very tightly in his sweater to stop him from scratching.

Ouch!

Hold STILL, Albert! Anyone'd think you weren't...

...pleased to see me!

When they got home, Chips put Albert down on the kitchen floor. Everyone gathered round, delighted.

Albert sniffed about a little, laid back his ears, and shook his back legs at them crossly. They gave him a big helping of tinned meat to celebrate, but he walked off, leaving most of it on the plate. The kitten finished it up.

That night they kept Albert indoors, shut in the kitchen with the kitten. But the next day he disappeared again. This time Chips knew just what to do.

He ran straight to Mrs Harris's shop. The first thing he saw was Albert, who was just finishing a large bowl of fishy left-overs.

Again Chips carried Albert home. This time Jessie helped. But before long Albert was back again at the fish-shop, sitting up by the till and eyeing a tray of fresh haddock. Three times they carried Albert back and three times he went missing, back to Mrs Harris. The fourth time was more than Chips could bear. He burst into tears.

Albert's forgotten he's supposed to be our cat!

Not AGAIN!

He likes being at the fish-shop better than being with US...

He thinks we don't love him any more!

Boo - hoooo!

Then Grandpa had a good idea. He suggested that they should ask Mrs Harris if *she* would like the kitten.

Albert will never want to stay under the same roof as that kitten. He can't stand the sight of it. Once it's gone, he'll soon come home to us, you'll see.

Do you really think so?

Sob!

So that was just what happened. Mrs Harris was quite delighted with the kitten. Because it was grey all over, and because Chips told her about how he had once thought the kitten was a ghost in his shopping-bag, she decided to call it Spook.

Oh, what a lovely little thing!

Dear little Spooky!

Here he is, Mrs Harris.

Grandpa was right. Albert was so disgusted to find Spook living at the fish-shop that he soon stopped going there, and settled down at home as though he'd never been away.

Dear old Albert!

Chips and Jessie often saw Spook when they went to Mrs Harris's shop. Mrs Harris fed him so many delicious fish meals that he soon grew from a little kitten to a very large cat with a glossy coat and handsome whiskers, much too solid and contented for a ghost!

WE WISH YOU
A MERRY
CHRISTMAS

Eight days to Christmas . . .

61

63